MY MOM'S PU...

Charlotte Hutchinson

illustrations by
Kathy R. Kaulbach

BLACK MOSS PRESS
WINDSOR, ONT.

My Mom's Purse

©Text 1991 Charlotte Hutchinson
©Illustrations 1991 Kathy R. Kaulbach

Published in 1991 by Black Moss Press at 1939
Alsace St., Windsor, Ontario, Canada,
N8W 1M5
Black Moss books are distributed in Canada
and the U.S. by Firefly Books, 250 Sparks
Ave., Willowdale, Ontario, Canada, M2H 2S4
All orders should be directed there.

Black Moss books are published in Canada
with the assistance of the Canada Council
and the Ontario Arts Council.

Canadian Cataloguing in Publication Data
Hutchinson, Charlotte, 1949-
My mom's purse

ISBN 0-88753-199-7

I. Kaulbach, Kathy R. (Kathy Rose), 1955-

II. Title.

PS8565.U83M64 1991   jC813'.54   C91-090271-2
PZ7.H88Mo 1991

With thanks to Roly, for the idea, and to
Jackie, Paul and Naomi for their special help

My mom has this really enormous purse with all sorts of stuff in it. My dad says it has everything in it from A to Z, except for the kitchen sink. Dad's right—there's no kitchen sink. That's silly anyway, but there really is everything from A to Z.

Mom carries my plastic airplane in her purse for me sometimes when we're out. I need it for my Indian when he's not riding the zebra. My mom carries them all for me if I'm busy doing something else.

She also carries Aspirin and Auntie Acid with her all the time. She says she couldn't be without them, having five kids and all. I don't know why—she never gives us any. But she always has two Auntie Acids instead of dessert when we go to our favourite restaurant. I snuck one once and I thought it tasted yucky. I'd rather have dessert.

Band-aids. Mom carries these around mostly for the twins. They're always falling down and hurting themselves—especially Johnnie. Big kids like me don't need them very often.

She has a comb in her purse. Whenever we go visiting, she has to comb everybody's hair. Janie, the other twin, always squiggles and squirms. And boy, did she ever yell the day she had gum caught in her hair and Mom didn't notice. That's when Mom started carrying scissors around with her, too.

She also has cards, a whole deck of them, in there. She and Dad use them for entertainment at night when we all go away on a trip together. Dad says they used to have other entertainment before we were all born.

She has to carry her driver's license, of course. That's big people stuff. I'm going to have one as soon as I'm old enough.

Mom jams in a whole bunch of diapers for the baby before we go out. Sometimes we have to come home before we want to just because she didn't take enough of them.

Elastics—lots of them. Mom ties Janie's hair back when she's eating. Otherwise, Janie gets all this food in her hair and it looks really gross.

Fingernail polish. Mom says the bottle in her purse is as old as the hills. She says she's keeping it as a souvenir. I don't know what she means. She tried to put some on yesterday, but the baby threw up when she was on the third nail. She says she's going to paint the other seven once the baby starts school.

And film. She always has a roll in her
purse that she has to take in for
developing. Mom's always taking
pictures of us. That's another time she
gets out the comb and has one of her
combing parties.

There's Gravol and gum in her purse. The gum's for my big brother and me. The Gravol's for the twins. They each get a tiny piece when we go on a long car trip. They usually fall asleep. That's a lot better than the time they threw up in the back seat.

Hairpins. Guess who these are for! Janie! Mom says that if there's even one loose strand of hair, Janie will manage to drag it through her food.

I already told you about my Indian. Then there's the iodine. Mom hauls that out and uses it before the Band-aids. You should hear Johnnie scream.

Brad says that just about everything in Mom's purse starts with "J" for "Junk". That's not true. There's lots of good stuff in there as well as the junk.

Keys, keys, lots of keys. Mom says that adults carry one key for every year of their age. She doesn't know what half of them are for, but she's scared to throw them out.

And then there's the Kleenex. Mom says she never goes anywhere with us kids without a purse full of Kleenex. She needs them for the twins and the baby.

Lipstick—that is one of the things I like best in Mom's purse. Sometimes she tries to put it on in the car and Dad pretends he has to stop suddenly. Is it ever neat! One time it made a red streak right into her nose! We nearly killed ourselves laughing—except for Mom.

One time Janie got hold of the lipstick. She tried to put it on like she'd seen Mom do. She looked like a clown in the circus. The Kleenex really came in handy that time.

Money, money, money. It's good for so many things—buying toys and treats and going to the movies and the carnival. Mom and Dad use it for other stuff, too. Dad keeps saying it doesn't grow on trees. I know that—leaves grow on trees.

Necklaces—Mom had three in her purse one day. She puts them on before she goes out, but she usually has to take them off because the baby bites and pulls at them. One day, her favourite one broke in the mall and the beads went everywhere. People were slipping and falling all over the place. Mom yelled at Brad and me to go pick them up, but we were laughing so much we could hardly move.

There may not be anything in Mom's purse that starts with "O" from now on. I put my ooze in there one day when I was through playing with it. Mom wasn't very happy when she found it. It took a long time for her to pick things out of it and wash them off. She says that from now on my ooze has to stay in my room.

This is boring stuff—pens, pencils
and paper. Mom's always writing stuff
down and making lists. I don't know
why she doesn't just remember things
like I do.

Quarters. Her purse is half full of quarters. She says she can't do without them. Brad's always asking for them so he can play the video games. She uses them in parking meters and to phone home to the baby sitter when she and Dad go out.

Mom puts the baby's rattle in her purse when the baby starts flinging it on the floor. I tell Mom that Samantha just wants to play. Mom says, well why don't I play with her, but I usually can't 'cause I'm too busy with my Indian.

I told you about the scissors. Mom also has a soother for the baby. I like it when the baby spits the soother out and giggles—then she cries if you don't put it back. Mom gets tired of it.

Toothbrush and toothpaste—more boring stuff. Mom carries them around with her, but she says she's so busy she hardly ever gets a chance to use them. I tried using that excuse, too, but it didn't work for me.

An umbrella. She has a collapsible one in her purse. You should see us all try to get under it. I'd rather just stay out in the rain, but oh, no, Mom won't let me. I might catch cold. One time Brad tripped me and I landed smack on top of Johnnie in a mud puddle. I could tell Mom wanted to yell really loudly, but she didn't 'cause we were out in public.

Mushy, gushy, yuk! Dad gave Mom this gigantic Valentine with birds, hearts and flowers all over it. It got covered with my ooze, but she cleaned it off and dried it out and put it back in her purse. I figure that's a waste of space.

Mom has a wallet of course—more adult stuff. But one day she had a bunch of Johnnie's worms in her purse, too. Just that once, though. She said the worms had to go! Sometimes mothers get upset over nothing. The worms were clean—Johnnie and Janie had licked them off.

Janie's xylophone. That's more wasted space. What a racket! Mom says it's better than having to listen to her scream and shout, though.

And Johnnie's yo-yo. He can't use it properly yet. It comes undone and gets all tangled up but he cries if he can't take it with him.

My zebra. I already mentioned that. My Indian rides it when he's in darkest Africa and there's no place for the plane to land.

Well, that's the story of my mom's purse. Sometimes my mom plays a game with me. She names a letter of the alphabet and I try to remember what's in her purse that starts with that letter. Sometimes we go through the whole alphabet from A to Z, like I just did for you.

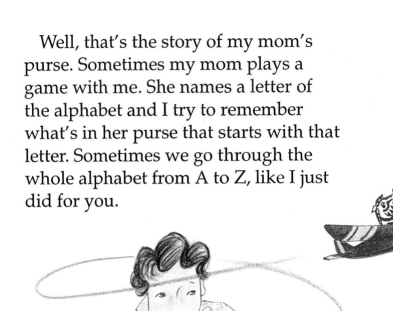

Do you remember what "O" was?